W9-AQK-227

MARVEL
SPIDEY
and his AMAZING FRIENDS

Super Hero Hiccups

Adapted by **Steve Behling**
Based on the episode written by **Ken Kristensen**
Illustrated by **Premise Entertainment**

Los Angeles • New York

Spidey and Miles
are Super Heroes.

Someone set off an alarm
at the library.

Miles sees
Green Goblin's glider.
He must be inside!

Miles can turn invisible.
He will sneak up
on Green Goblin!

Spidey and Miles head
inside.

Miles sees Green Goblin
reading a book.

Green Goblin reads about
a legendary warrior,
the Pumpkin King.

Green Goblin wants the
Pumpkin King's Power Sword!
It can destroy anything.

The heroes try to stop
Green Goblin.
But Miles has hiccups!

Green Goblin throws
pumpkin pranks!

Miles tries to thwip a web.
But he hiccups again!

Green Goblin leaves
to find the Power Sword.

Miles thinks his hiccups
ruined everything.
But Spidey says it is okay.

Spidey says, "When a plan doesn't go my way, I just try something else to save the day!"

Miles feels better.
"We must find the Power Sword
before Goblin does," Miles says.

Spidey takes a picture
of the book Goblin was reading.
Maybe they will find a clue!

The heroes go to WEB-Quarters.
Ghost-Spider looks for clues.
Can she find the Power Sword?

But Miles still has hiccups.
He almost zaps his friends
with his Arachno-sting!

Ghost-Spider finds
the Power Sword.
It is at the museum!

Miles wants to stay.
He thinks his hiccups
will cause trouble.

But even with his hiccups,
Miles can still help!

The team goes to the museum. They will get the Power Sword before Green Goblin does!

The heroes get the sword.
But Green Goblin takes it!

Miles still has hiccups.
But he must save his friends!

Miles uses his invisibility power.
He pretends to be a ghost!

Miles hiccups and zaps again.
Green Goblin is very afraid.
He thinks it's a *real* ghost!

Green Goblin drops the sword.
Miles takes the Power Sword!

Miles frees his friends
with the Power Sword.

Green Goblin tries to escape.
But the Spidey Team
catches him in their webs!

The Spidey Team wins.
And Miles's hiccups are gone!

But now Green Goblin
has hiccups!
Sorry, Goblin!